A Christmas Prayer

How Noah and Sarah
Saved Christmas

Maria Loewen

Illustrated By: Schenker De Leon

WestBow Press books may be ordered through booksellers or by contacting:

WestBow Press
A Division of Thomas Nelson & Zondervan
1663 Liberty Drive
Bloomington, IN 47403
www.westbowpress.com
1 (866) 928-1240

Because of the dynamic nature of the Internet, any web addresses or links contained in this book may have changed since publication and may no longer be valid. The views expressed in this work are solely those of the author and do not necessarily reflect the views of the publisher, and the publisher hereby disclaims any responsibility for them.

Any people depicted in stock imagery provided by Getty Images are models, and such images are being used for illustrative purposes only. Certain stock imagery © Getty Images.

ISBN: 978-1-9736-2029-7 (sc)
ISBN: 978-1-9736-2030-3 (e)

Library of Congress Control Number: 2018902066

Print information available on the last page.

WestBow Press rev. date: 02/23/2018

WESTBOW
PRESS®
A DIVISION OF THOMAS NELSON
& ZONDERVAN

Long ago, two siblings, Noah and Sarah, were on a hunt to save Christmas. It all started when Sarah and Noah ran along the snow-covered boardwalk, like any other day. Until they came to the general store. They were just about to enter the store when they overheard Mom talking to the clerk about the stage couch. Sarah and Noah looked at each other, then marched into the store.

"The stage can't come in? Why not?" Noah eagerly waited for an answer.

"There's a huge storm some ways off from here; the stage can't make it through the storm." Brian, the store clerk, answered.

"What does that mean?" Sarah asked.

"It means all the stuff people bought for Christmas won't make it hear in time." Mom answered.

"What about Daddy? Won't he be here for Christmas?" Sarah asked.

"I'm afraid not." Mom brushed Sarah's hair out of her eyes.

Noah looked down to his toes, thinking to himself, *'What kind of Christmas would this be? No presents, no Christmas dinner . . . and no Dad for Christmas.'* Noah felt a deep sense of sadness in his heart.

For the rest of the day Noah was quiet. He sat on the front porch steps, petting his dog, until his sister Sarah came outside.

"What's wrong Noah?" Sarah sat down beside the dog.

"You know I was thinking . . . Mom looked really sad when she heard the stage wasn't coming."

"I think she was sadder that Daddy can't come home for Christmas." Sarah mentioned.

"Yes, but don't you think if we had supplies for a Christmas dinner she would be happier? I'm going to go look for a turkey. I remember where Dad always goes hunting and it shouldn't take very long to find a turkey."

"With what are you going to shoot it?" Sarah couldn't believe her older brother would try something like this . . . and all by himself!

"With my sling shot." Noah replied.

"I'm going with you!" Sarah would not let her brother out of sight.

"OK. We'll leave two days from today—the day before Christmas. When we go, put lots of cloths on because it'll be cold." Then Noah stood up and walked inside.

Two days later, Noah and Sarah put on their thickest mittens and coats, along with their best snow boots. Noah put his sling shot in his pocket and they marched outside. Noah often played in the woods behind their house, so their mom let them go; although, she didn't know they were on a hunt for the biggest turkey in the woods.

"We don't need to be scared Sarah. I have played here before, it's not that far from our house. And Mom knows where we're at. And besides, Mom always says Jesus is with us everywhere we go." Noah comforted Sarah.

"Yes, I believe it's true. Especially now that it's only a day till His birthday. Don't you think?" Sarah asked Noah, while following him into the woods.

"Maybe so." Noah replied.

They didn't talk for a while after that, until they found the perfect turkey. It was a big one!

"Ssshhh . . . be very still Sarah," Noah whispered.

Sarah didn't move an inch. Noah slowly pulled out his sling shot and grabbed the smoothest stone from his pocket. He gently placed it in his sling shot and put it up against his eye. He made sure his aim was right on target, and then, v-o-o-m-m-m, the stone flew and hit the turkey right on the head.

"You got it!" Sarah yelled in excitement and all the other turkeys ran away, but their turkey staid right there, laying on the ground.

They ran up to the turkey and looked at it to make sure it was safe to pick up. Finally, Noah grabbed it by the legs and they began to walk home.

"Mom will like this for dinner tonight," Noah said.

Sarah agreed and walked beside Noah, hands in her pockets.

"You know Sarah," Noah said, "I don't think I shot this turkey."

"But it fell right when you shot!"

"Yes, but didn't you hear the gun shot?" Noah thought very hard about how they could have gotten such a big turkey with such a little sling shot.

"You think Jesus helped us get the turkey?" Sarah's eyes grew big in excitement. Sarah thought that would be the coolest thing ever!

"Like a Bible story!" She said.

"Yes, something like that." Noah pondered over the idea. "Either way I'm glad we got the turkey for Mom."

Later that afternoon, Noah and Sarah helped the town's people decorate the big Christmas tree, that stood right in the middle of main street where everyone could see it. They sung, laughed and cheered, when Noah noticed Brain slip away from the group and walk toward the store. Noah was tempted to follow Brian, yet thought he should probably respect his privacy. So, he focused on decorating the tree.

When all the decorating was done everyone walked to their houses, wishing each other a Merry Christmas. Yet, all Sarah and Noah wished for now was that their Dad would make it home for Christmas. However, it was Christmas eve and the stage couch still hadn't come in.

When Noah and Sarah went outside to get firewood they had an idea.

"Come on Noah, lets pray. Maybe Daddy will come home then." Sarah dropped the firewood and grabbed Noah's hand.

"Okay," Noah agreed, and they bowed their heads in prayer.

Noah prayed that everyone in town would have a blessed Christmas and a warm, cozy home to celebrate in, but most of all, that their Dad would make it home for Christmas. When they looked up and opened their eyes, they saw fluffy snowflakes drifting to the ground. They reached out their hands and let the snow melt on their mittens. They laughed and danced in the snow. Soon the fresh green Christmas tree had specks of white everywhere and the horses snorted, as the icy drops landed on their noses.

When Mom called dinner they all gathered around the table and said grace. Mom prepared the best Christmas dinner they had ever seen. The only one that was missing was their Dad, who always sat at the end of the table. And after the meal he would read the Christmas story, but . . . not tonight. Noah and Sarah didn't even care about the bare spot underneath the Christmas tree, all their presents didn't matter to them now.

Mom was just about to put mash potatoes in Sarah's plate when someone knocked at the door. Noah got up and ran to the door, when he opened it he saw Brian standing in front of the door, with his horse and sled parked in front of the porch. Noah grabbed his coat and stepped out on the porch, closing the door behind him.

"Merry Christmas!" Brian smiled at Noah, then handed him a brown package and a bag that had every kind of candy in the store.

"Where did you get this?" Noah asked.

"Oh, there were a few things left in the old general store." Brian smiled at Noah.

"Thank you!" Noah loved candy, yet he couldn't help but ask, "Dad still hasn't come?"

"Actually . . ." Brian started to talk, but then around the corner came a big, strong man, known as Noah and Sarah's dad.

"Dad!" Noah ran up to him and when Sarah heard what Noah said she came running too.

"How did you get home" Sarah asked?

"I hitched a ride with a traveler that was headed this way." Dad answered, smiling at them.

They both hugged their dad. Smiling at each other, knowing God had heard their prayer.

Mom, Dad, Noah and Sarah wished Brian a Merry Christmas and went inside. Once inside Noah and Sarah ran to the window and waved at Brain. Brain winked at them, and his horse trotted down the street, while he rode behind in his sled.

Later that night, when it stopped snowing and the moon came out from its hiding place; far up in the sky shone a bright star over the little town. Noah and Sarah thought it was God's light shining over all his people, on Christmas Eve.

The End.

Printed in the United States
By Bookmasters